MA

Miss Mary Mack

You can play this simple hand-clapping game when you sing "Miss Mary Mack." Find a partner and face him or her. Both of you should carry out the actions described below as you sing.

1. Cross arms in front of chest.

2. Slap thighs.

3. Clap.

4. Clap your right hand against your partner's right hand.

5. Clap on rest.

6. Clap your left hand against your partner's left hand.

7. Clap on rest.

8. Clap your right hand against your partner's right hand.

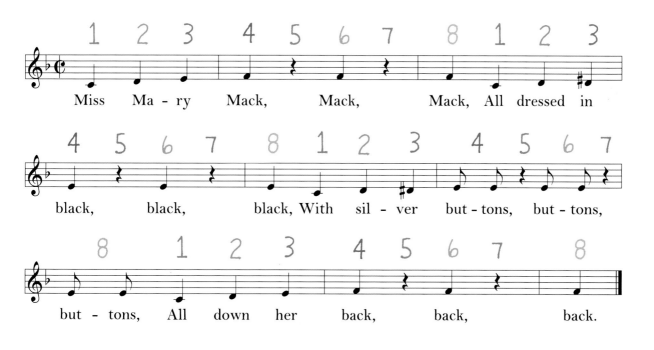

Miss Ma - ry Mack, Mack, Mack, All dressed in

black, black, black, With sil - ver but - tons, but - tons,

but - tons, All down her back, back, back.

To Alix and Cori Hoberma
and Joshua Lawrence
— M. A. H.

To Becky Westcott, with lo
— N. B. W.

Text copyright © 1998 by Mary Ann Hoberman
Illustrations copyright © 1998 by Nadine Bernard Westcott
More fun with Miss Mary Mack! Activity Page © 2003 by
Little, Brown and Company (Inc.)
Sing-Along Stories Series Editor, Mary Ann Hoberman

First Paperback Edition

The Sing-Along Stories logo design is a trademark of
Little, Brown and Company (Inc.).

Library of Congress Cataloging-in-Publication Data

Hoberman, Mary Ann.
   Miss Mary Mack : a hand-clapping rhyme / adapted by Mary Ann
Hoberman ; illustrated by Nadine Bernard Westcott. — 1st ed.
      p.   cm.
   Summary: An expanded adaptation of the familiar hand-clapping
rhyme about a young girl and an elephant.
   ISBN 0-316-93118-7 (hc)/ISBN 0-316-07614-7 (pb)
   1. Nursery rhymes.   2. Children's poetry.   [1. Nursery rhymes.]
I. Westcott, Nadine Bernard, ill.   II. Title.
PZ8.3.H66Mi 1998
398'.8—dc20   96-34829

HC: 10 9 8 7 6 5

PB: 10 9 8 7 6 5 4 3 2 1

SC

Printed in Hong Kong

Miss Mary Mack

Adapted by
Mary Ann Hoberman

Illustrated by
Nadine Bernard Westcott

Sing-Along Stories Series Editor, Mary Ann Hoberman

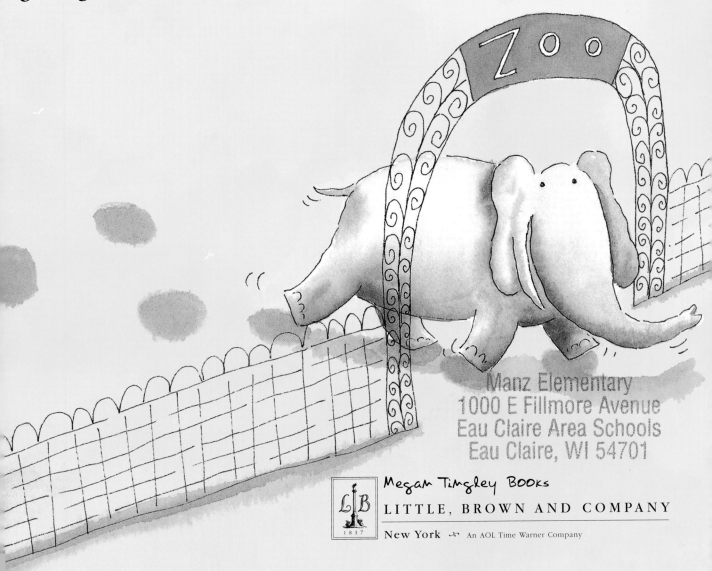

Megan Tingley Books
LITTLE, BROWN AND COMPANY
New York · An AOL Time Warner Company

Miss Mary Mack, Mack, Mack,
All dressed in black, black, black,
With silver buttons, buttons, buttons,
All down her back, back, back.

She asked her mother, mother, mother,
For fifty cents, cents, cents,
To see the elephant, elephant, elephant,
Jump the fence, fence, fence.

He jumped so high, high, high,
He reached the sky, sky, sky,
And didn't come back, back, back,
Till the fourth of July, July, July.

He fell so fast, fast, fast,
He fell so hard, hard, hard,
He made a hole, hole, hole,
In her back yard, yard, yard.

The catsup splashed, splashed, splashed,
The soda popped, popped, popped,
The people screamed, screamed, screamed,
The picnic stopped, stopped, stopped.

POP!

POP!

POP!

He landed with, with, with,
A bumpy thud, thud, thud,
And got all full, full, full,
Of muck and mud, mud, mud.

Miss Mary Mack, Mack, Mack,
Gave him a drink, drink, drink,
And he got clean, clean, clean,
Quick as a wink, wink, wink.

His keeper came, came, came,
To take him back, back, back,
"Oh, please don't go, go, go,"
Cried Mary Mack, Mack, Mack.

"I'll feed you hay, hay, hay,
And peanut tea, tea, tea,
If you will stay, stay, stay,
And live with me, me, me.

"The silver buttons, buttons, buttons,
Down my dress, dress, dress,
Will all be yours, yours, yours,
If you say yes, yes, yes."

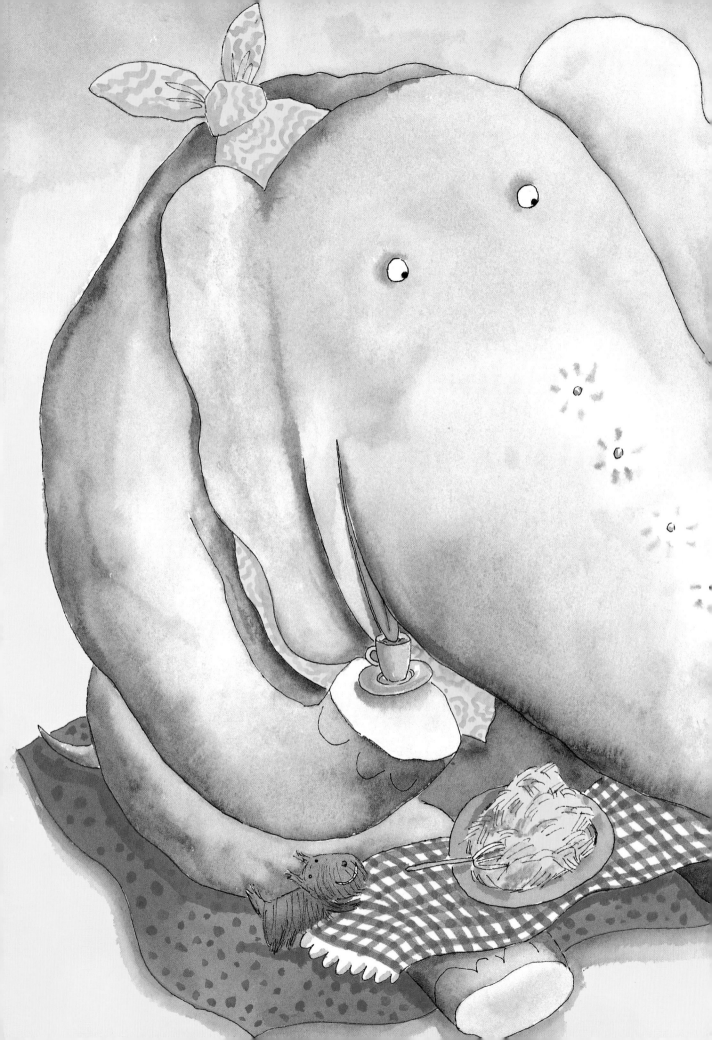

Now Mary Mack, Mack, Mack,
All dressed in black, black, black,
Has *purple* buttons, buttons, buttons,
Down her back, back, back.

And Elephant, Phant, Phant,
Has shiny rows, rows, rows,
Of silver buttons, buttons, buttons,
Down his nose, nose, nose.

And every day, day, day,
For fifty cents, cents, cents,
They both go out, out, out,
And jump the fence, fence, fence!

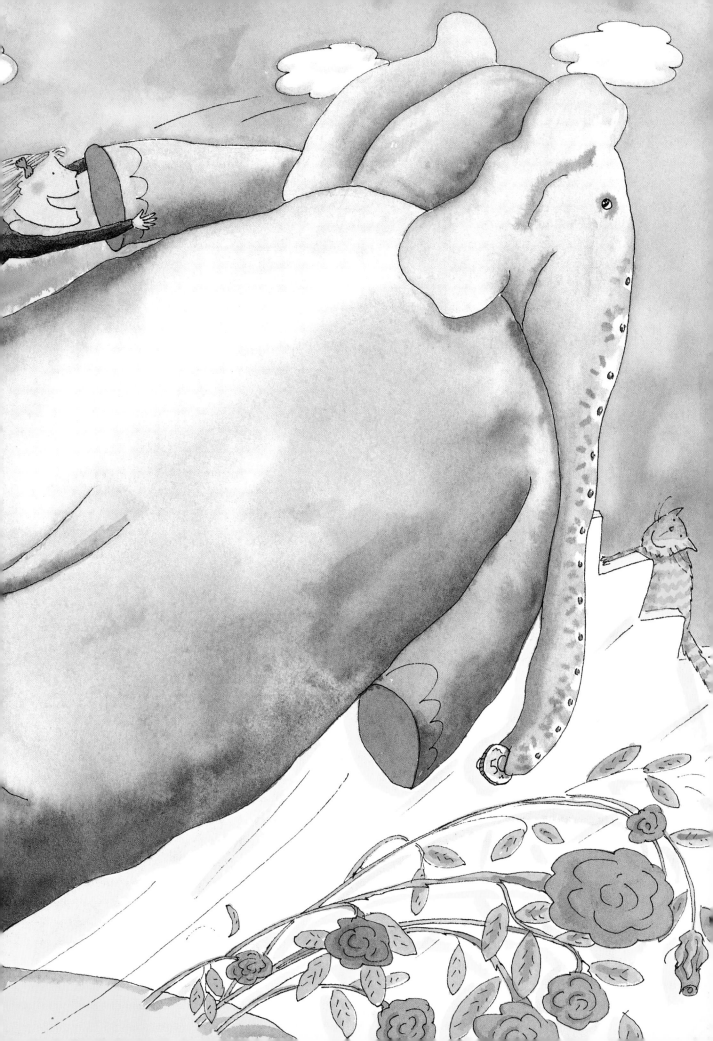

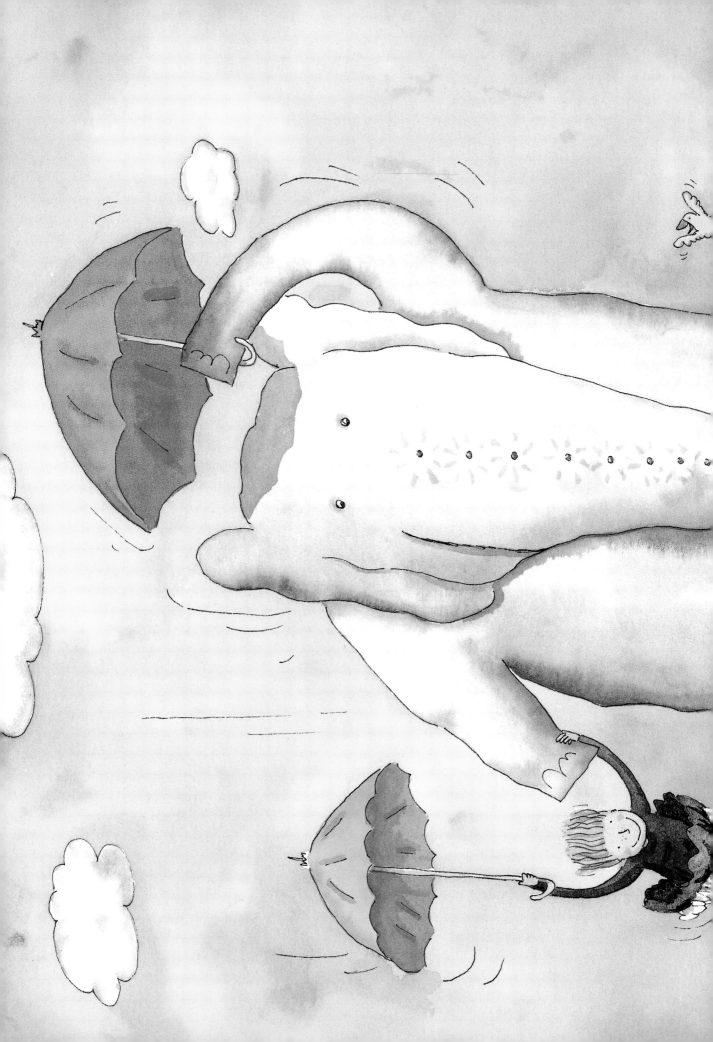

More fun with *Miss Mary Mack!*

♪   ♪   ♪

1 Sing and read *Miss Mary Mack* with a friend, parent, or teacher. What other words can you think of that rhyme with "Mack" besides "black" and "back"?

2 The elephant didn't come back until the Fourth of July! Discuss why the Fourth of July is America's birthday. Make an American flag and share special things that you do with your family on this holiday.

3 Draw a picture and write a short rhyme substituting your name or a friend's name for Miss Mary Mack's name and your favorite zoo animal for the elephant.

4 Miss Mary Mack paid fifty cents to see the elephant. Can you think of different ways to make fifty cents (using quarters, dimes, nickels, and pennies)? Practice counting using buttons, coins, and peanuts.

5 Plan a picnic or tea party. Invite guests to wear clothes with buttons, and serve "elephant snacks" like peanut butter sandwiches and peanut butter cookies!